PICTURE BOOKS BY SUSAN COOPER

The Selkie Girl
The Silver Cow: A Welsh Tale
Tam Lin
All illustrated by Warwick Hutton
(MARGARET K. MCELDERRY BOOKS)

for
Kira and Denny
Chrissie and Amy
and of course
Matthew

S.C.

to
Kari, Joe, and Emily,
who gave me
three new sets of eyes
for looking at the world

J.A.S.

Aladdin Paperbacks
An imprint of Simon & Schuster
Children's Publishing Division
1230 Avenue of the Americas
New York, NY 10020
Text copyright © 1991 by Susan Cooper
Illustrations copyright © 1991 by Jos. A. Smith

First Aladdin Paperbacks edition, 1994
Printed in Hong Kong by South China Printing Company (1988) Ltd.
10 9 8 7 6 5
A hardcover edition of *Matthew's Dragon* is available from Margaret K. McElderry Books.

Library of Congress Cataloging-in-Publication Data
Cooper, Susan.
Matthew's dragon / Susan Cooper ; illustrated by Jos. A. Smith. — 1st Aladdin Books ed.
p.   cm.
Summary: The dragon in Matthew's picture book comes to life and takes him for an
amazing nocturnal ride.
ISBN 0-689-71794-6
[1. Dragons—Fiction.] I. Smith, Joseph A. (Joseph Anthony), 1936– ill. II. Title.
PZ7.C7878Mat 1994
[E]—dc20 93-26574

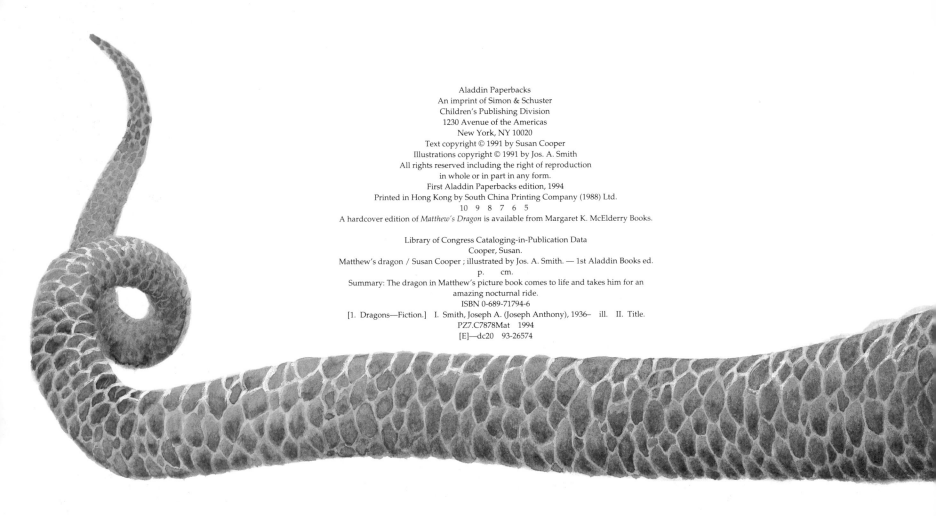

Matthew's Dragon

Susan Cooper
illustrated by Jos. A. Smith

ALADDIN PAPERBACKS

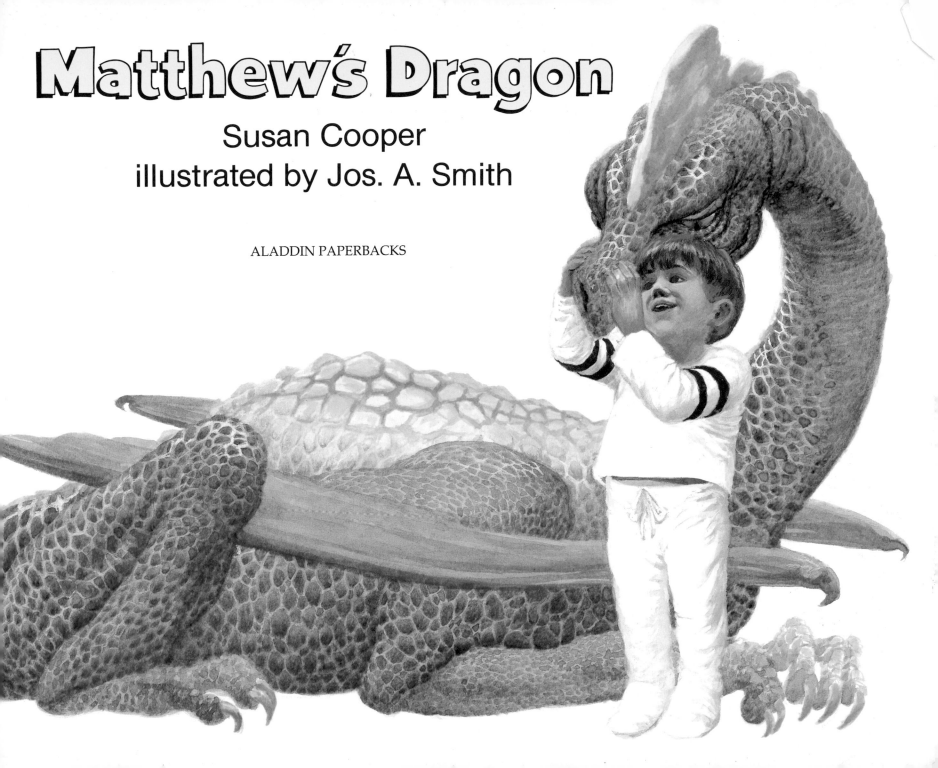

atthew's mother was sitting on his bed, reading him a bedtime story. She had just turned the last page.

"And so the dragon flew back to his castle, and pulled up the drawbridge, and went to sleep," she read.

She held up the picture of the sleeping dragon to show Matthew, and closed the book.

"Just one more," said Matthew hopefully. All his favorite stories were about dragons.

His mother said firmly, "Tomorrow." She put the book on the bedside table and tucked him in. "Good night, Matt. Sleep tight."

Matthew sighed. "'Night." He snuggled down, as his mother kissed the top of his head and turned out the lamp. The door closed behind her. In the dark room, Matthew shut his eyes—and then he opened them again. He gasped.

The cover of the book on the bedside table was moving gently up and down, and a green light was shining out of the pages.

Very cautiously, Matthew reached out his hand from under the blankets, and with one finger he pushed up the cover. As the book opened, the green light flooded into the room, and from the picture on the last page, the dragon sat up and grinned at him.

"I *didn't* go to sleep," the dragon said, in a surprisingly deep voice. He was a small but extremely beautiful dragon. Matthew recognized him instantly. His skin was bright green, the scales on his back and tail were golden, and his eyes shone red as rubies. "I don't *want* to go to sleep," the dragon said. "Do you?"

Matthew stared at him. "No!" he said hastily. "Oh no, I don't, not at all!"

"Come on, then," the dragon said. He reached out one shining golden claw. Matthew pushed back the blankets—and suddenly he was as small as the dragon, standing beside him on a sloping white floor that was the page of the book. Dazed, he took the outstretched golden claw, and the dragon swung him up so that he was sitting on his back, between the handsome gold-crested head and the curving green wings.

"Hold tight," said the dragon, and he took off from the bedside table and glided to the windowsill, where Matthew's mother always left the window open a few inches to let in fresh air.

Outside the window Matthew could see a silvery curved bridge stretching into the night. It arched through the air and down to the ground, glinting in the moonlight. "It's your drawbridge!" he said.

"Get off my back, or you'll bang your head," said the dragon.
Together they slipped out under the window, and onto the
shining bridge, and ran down, down, down into the garden.

When Matthew looked back, the bridge had disappeared. All he could
see was the big full moon high in the sky, above the dark shape
of the maple tree that grew out of the lawn—and all around him,
enormous blades of grass wider than his hand and higher than his
head. Now that he was a very small person, it was not so easy to
walk across the lawn.

"Come on!" said the dragon. He pushed boldly through the
forest of grass, and Matthew fought his way after him.

"Dragon! Where are we going?"

"For a little bedtime snack," the dragon said happily.

The grass ended, and they were facing a huge empty expanse of grey rocks, each one as big as Matthew's head. Matthew stared. It was the gravel path leading to his father's greenhouse.

He started out across it, but he heard the dragon give a sudden loud shriek, a strange rusty sound like the hoot of a train—and a dragon-wing knocked him sprawling back into the grass as a great black shape hurtled over their heads.

"Quick!" The dragon pulled him to his feet and they ran, stumbling over the grey rocks. "Quick, quick!" Matthew tried to look over his shoulder, but the dragon pulled him sideways through a thin black gap between two towering white walls.

The black cat chasing them, big as a horse, crashed into the door of the greenhouse and snarled with rage.

Matthew and the dragon were safe inside the greenhouse. The door was open just a crack, just enough for them. Not enough for the cat.

The dragon said cheerfully, "He thought we were *his* bedtime snack. Well, we're not."

"That's the cat next door," Matthew said. "He's mean. I saw him catch a bird once and play with it like a tennis ball, and then he killed it."

"Come on," the dragon said. He took hold of a strand of ivy dangling from the greenhouse shelf, and began to climb up it. Matthew struggled up after him, and when he got to the top he found the dragon perched triumphantly on the edge of a large flowerpot. The pot held one of Matthew's father's dwarf tomato plants, his pride and joy. He had grown six of them, all standing in a row, and all covered with delicious little cherry tomatoes.

"Snack time," said the dragon. He reached up a claw and picked a bright red cherry tomato, which to Matthew now seemed the size of a large grapefruit. "Excellent," said the dragon with his mouth full. "Full of vitamin C. Good for the wings."

Matthew had no wings, but he ate a tomato, just to be friendly. The dragon ate six. Then he sighed contentedly, and burped. "Any sign of the cat?" he said.

Matthew peered out at the moonlit garden. It was much larger than usual, but empty; nothing moved.

"All clear," he said.

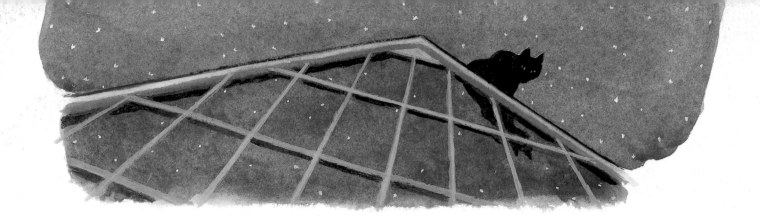

They climbed to the ground again and slipped cautiously out through the greenhouse door. Matthew breathed the cool night air; he smelled honeysuckle.

But although Matthew couldn't see it, the cat was still there. Fat and greedy, lightfooted and sly, it lurked on the edge of the greenhouse roof, watching, waiting. It saw their moving figures. The dragon looked prickly, it decided, but that other one looked smooth and tasty: a very nice mouthful, like a large mouse....

It leaped. Matthew shouted in terror as the diving black shape knocked him to the ground, trapping him under one fierce paw. He was caught. He couldn't move. He stared up horrified into the gleaming yellow eyes, the grinning mouth full of pointed white teeth.

The cat crouched, triumphant, gloating. First it would play with this creature, like a tennis ball. And then—

Knocked end over end by the cat's jump, the dragon turned a final somersault and landed on his feet. He stood still, watching the cat. His eyes began to glow red as cherry tomatoes, and he took a deep, deep breath—and he began to grow.

He grew and he grew; as big as the cat, as big as the greenhouse, as big as the house. He towered over the garden; his great shape darkened the sky, blotted out the moon. He was so huge that neither Matthew nor the cat knew that he was there. Lying terrified between the cat's paws, Matthew knew only that a great golden claw came down out of the sky, hooked itself into the belt of his pajama pants and lifted him upward.

The cat arched its spine, hissing.

The dragon swung Matthew up onto his back, to sit on his scaly neck between the handsome gold-crested head and the curving green wings. Then he reached his golden claw down again and picked up the cat. He swung it to and fro, slowly, twenty feet in the air.

The cat yowled, terrified. The dragon went on swinging, and the yowling became a shriek.

Light streamed across the dark lawn as Matthew's father opened the back door of the house. "Go home, you stupid cat!" he yelled.

High on the dragon's back, Matthew held his breath; but his father saw nothing. The dragon was so big now that he filled as much of the sky as the tall maple tree that grew out of the lawn.

The back door closed.

The dragon swung the yowling cat over to a big barrel that collected rainwater from the greenhouse roof. He dropped the cat in, with a splash. Matthew cheered.

"Hold on," the dragon said. And he flew.

Higher and higher he flew in the night sky, curving round and around in a long rising spiral, his green wings spread huge and silent. The stars grew brighter as he rose closer to them. Far below, the lights of Matthew's town were spread like bright necklaces, glittering. And as he flew, the dragon sang.

He sang a long wordless music, like the singing of the wind, like the singing of the sea. Matthew clung to his gold-scaled neck and listened in delight, and gradually he began to hear other voices, faint, growing, joining in. He peered out at the moon-washed sky, and saw stars that were not stars; moving lights that grew larger and swooped closer. He saw then that they were dragons.

From every part of the sky the dragons came flying, turning,
banking; sweeping over and under Matthew's dragon as if to greet
him. All the time their voices rose and fell in unison, mysterious,
beautiful, filling the sky with dragonsong. And not one of them
looked the same as any other. They were all colors and shapes and
sizes: there were red dragons or green, silver or gold or steely grey;
there were dragons with spiny iron claws, or dragons feathered soft
as rainbows. For these, Matthew realized, were all the dragons ever
put into the world of story.

Every dragon ever imagined was here, swirling round the sky;
every dragon that ever was. Matthew lay with his arms around his
own dragon's neck, and laughed aloud. They were all different, and
he recognized them all. The horizon tilted as his dragon banked left
and then right, and like great gleaming birds all the other dragons
swooped about him in a shifting cloud.

Then their music began to fade, and they fell into line so that they were flying in the long wonderful arrowhead shape in which wild geese fly, or wild ducks or swans. The long V of their arrowhead filled the whole sky, and Matthew and his dragon flew at the tip, leading all the rest.

Matthew's dragon lifted his golden-crested head, and called out with the same long dragon-call that Matthew had heard before—the long rusty hoot like the sound of a distant train. One by one the other dragons hooted in return, calling in farewell, and one by one they banked away and disappeared into the wide sky.

The dragon looked over his shoulder at Matthew. "*Now* I think I might go to sleep," he said. "How about you?"

Matthew saw the glimmering curve of the drawbridge coming closer as they dropped through the night. Suddenly he gave a huge yawn. "Well, maybe," he said.

As they came to the shining bridge that led to Matthew's bedroom, all at once they were the right size to walk across it and in through the open window. From the windowsill, Matthew glanced down at the house next door, and on the doorstep he saw a very wet and sulky cat licking itself. He grinned.

"Thank you, dragon," he said.

"They were very good tomatoes," the dragon said.

So Matthew climbed into bed, and Matthew's dragon climbed back inside the book and curled himself up into the picture he had come from.

"'Night, dragon," said Matthew.

"Good night, Matthew," said the dragon. "See you tomorrow."

And Matthew closed the book very gently, and they both went to sleep.